Dinos Whodunnit?

WORLD'S
BIGGEST
DINOSAUR
EGG

Written by Jane Langford
Illustrated by David Mostyn

CHAPTER ONE

Tom and Mollie run up the steps of the museum. Today is the first day of the dinosaur exhibition.

The lady at the desk speaks to Tom and Mollie.

Have you come to see the dinosaurs?

Yes, please.

Tom and Mollie go in. A strange man goes in after them.

Go on in.

The lady at the desk picks up the phone.

Hello, security?

Just to let you know, that man is here again.

I'll keep an eye on him.

Tom and Mollie look at the dinosaurs.

Look at those teeth!

All the better to eat you with!

The Head of Security looks at the strange man.

Here again, Sir?

Yes, I really like museums.

Tom and Mollie like the dinosaurs.

The Head of Security doesn't like the strange man.

A crowd of people push past Tom and Mollie.

Stand back for the Mayor!

Excuse me!

The people go into a little room. Tom and Mollie follow them.

SPECIAL EXHIBIT

Where are they all going?

The Head of Security follows the strange
man into the little room.

Quiet please,
everyone.

SPECIAL EXHIBIT

What's in there?

I don't know.

A TV man points his camera at a big case. The case is in the middle of the room and everyone is looking at it.

What's in the case?

I don't know.

Is it a dinosaur?

I can't tell! It's got a big cloth over it.

CHAPTER TWO

The TV camera zooms in.
The Mayor starts to speak again.

You can take photographs,
but please do not touch.

The case is protected by laser beams
and by our Head of Security.

Everyone pushes forward to get a better look.

The TV man is pushed into the Mayor.
The Mayor is pushed into Mollie.

Mollie falls into the path of the laser beams.

Red lights flash. Alarm bells ring.

Security men come running into the little room.

The Head of Security is very cross.

The Head of Security takes a key out of his pocket.

I'll turn this.

Will it turn off the red lights?

Yes.

And will the alarm bells stop ringing?

Yes.

The Head of Security turns the key. The red lights stop flashing. And the alarm bells stop ringing.

Phew!

That's better!

But something else happens as well.

Mollie is scared. So is Tom.

Someone speaks.

Stand still, everyone.

It is the Head of Security.

I will turn the lights back on.

Mollie feels someone push past her.

Ow! Someone scratched me!

Suddenly the lights come on. Everybody gasps.
The dinosaur egg has gone! So has the strange man.

CHAPTER THREE

Tom and Mollie look at the empty case.
They gasp in horror.

The egg has gone!

Oh, no!

Someone must have taken it!

TOILETS

The Head of Security looks at Tom and Mollie.

Did you take it?

No, we didn't!

TOILETS

Yes, you did!

You were the closest.

And you set off the alarms.

Tom and Mollie are very scared. Everyone is looking at them.

We didn't take it.

Suddenly the Mayor screams.

My bag has gone!

The Head of Security looks at the Mayor.

Was there much in it?

The Mayor stops screaming and thinks for a moment.

Yes, my lunch was in the bag.

Wait a minute. I ate my lunch, so the bag was empty.

The Head of Security is very puzzled.

Who would want to steal an empty bag?

The thief of course!

Why?

They could put the egg in the bag.

Then run away with it.

Everyone stares at Tom and Mollie.

The Head of Security looks at Tom and Mollie.

I still think it was you.

He takes them out to the desk.

Call the police!

But we didn't do anything!

Then Mollie sees something out of the corner of her eye. Suddenly she shouts.

But do you?
Go on, guess whodunnit!

Solution: *it was the lady at the desk*

Clues

1 She has a newspaper on her desk with a headline:
American offers £1,000,000 for world's largest egg.
She has circled it (page 4).

2 She is eating a chocolate bar (page 5). She drops the
wrapper by the case (page 21).

3 She pushes the TV man and he pushes the Mayor. Then
the Mayor pushes Mollie into the laser beams (page 14).

4 She turns the lights off. We can see her hand creeping
round the door frame to turn them off (page 18).

5 She is the only one with long nails. So *she* must
have scratched Mollie (page 20).

6 The straps of the missing bag are hanging out of her
filing cabinet (page 30).

7 The strange man is obviously a suspect. He disappears on
page 18 just before the egg is stolen. But on page 28 he is
seen coming out of the toilets, so he couldn't have stolen
the egg.